Handsome Hog

First published in 2009 by Hodder Children's Books
This paperback edition published in 2010

Text copyright © Bruce Hobson 2009
Illustrations copyright © Adrienne Kennaway 2009
www.brucehobson.net

Hodder Children's Books, 338 Euston Road, London, NW1 3BH

Hodder Children's Books Australia
Level 17/207 Kent Street, Sydney, NSW 2000

A catalogue record of this book is available from the British Library.

ISBN: 978 0 340 97035 5

Printed in China

Hodder Children's Books is a division of Hachette Children's Books.
An Hachette UK Company.
www.hachette.co.uk

HANDSOME HOG

Written by
Mwenye Hadithi

Illustrated by
Adrienne Kennaway

h
Hodder
Children's
Books

A division of Hachette Children's Books

On the Great Grassy African Plain,
where the Candlestick Cactus grew,
lived Handsome Hog.

He had a beautiful smooth coat of the finest brown hair, and his extremely elegant tail swished to and fro when he ran.

One day Prickly Porcupine, who was very prickly and not pretty at all, was digging a large hole to sleep in. She was thirsty after her hard work so she went to the river for a drink.

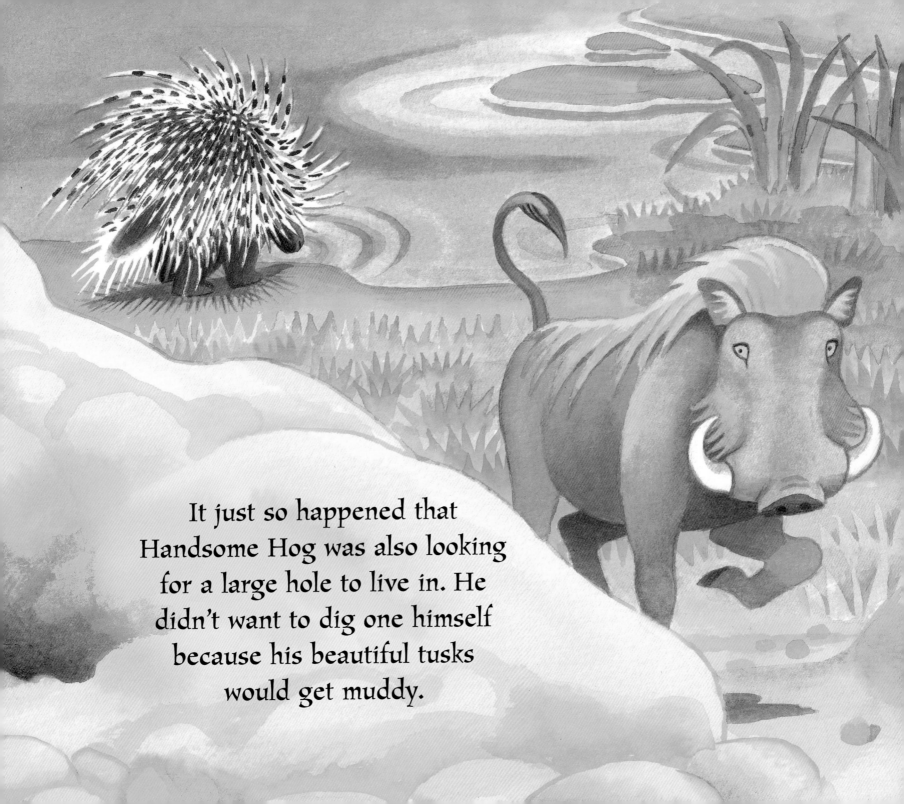

It just so happened that Handsome Hog was also looking for a large hole to live in. He didn't want to dig one himself because his beautiful tusks would get muddy.

Handsome Hog found the empty hole dug by Porcupine, and
Hog and Mrs Hog and all the little baby hogs moved in. Just like that.

When Porcupine returned to her hole it was full of big hogs and little hogs.

"But I am the one who dug this splendid hole!" complained Porcupine.

"Well, it's mine now, you ugly creature," said Hog rudely.

"Go away!"

That evening Handsome Hog and his family trotted off to the river. They greeted Colobus Monkey and Leopard and all the other beautiful animals as they gathered for a drink.

But they didn't talk to the funny-looking animals, and they especially didn't talk to Porcupine.

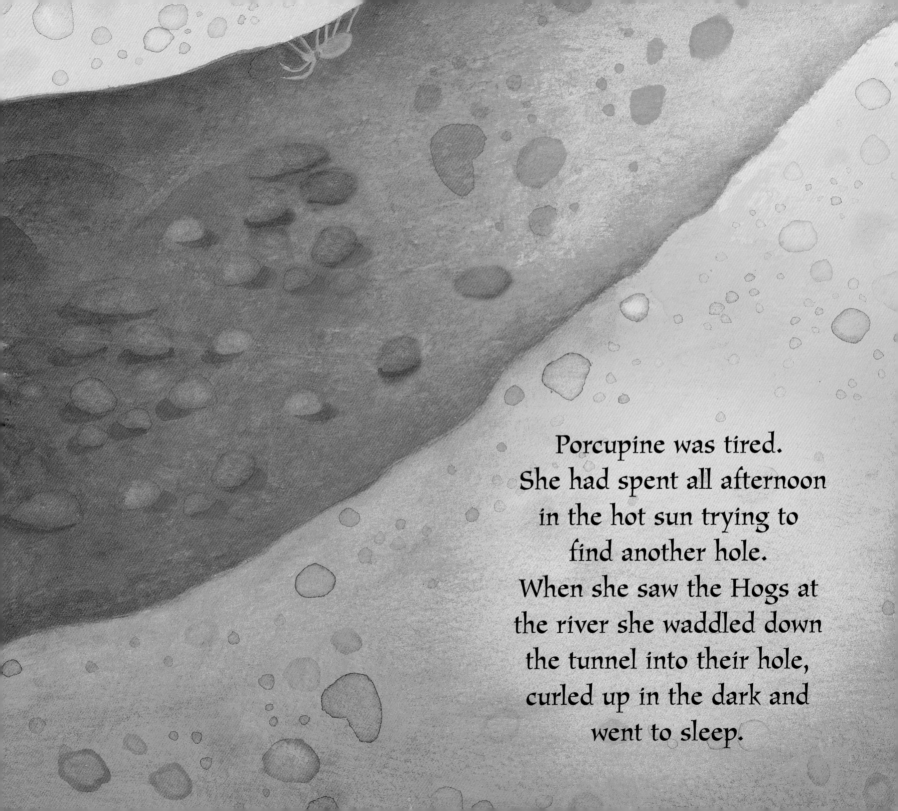

Porcupine was tired.
She had spent all afternoon
in the hot sun trying to
find another hole.
When she saw the Hogs at
the river she waddled down
the tunnel into their hole,
curled up in the dark and
went to sleep.

Handsome Hog trotted back and forth by the water's edge, imagining what the other animals were saying.

"There goes Handsome Hog!"

"What fine-looking fur!"

"What an elegant tail!"

Lion arrived to take a drink. His huge mane was all fluffed up by the wind.

"Such untidy hair," murmured Hog, admiring his own smooth head. Lion growled and walked off.

After Lion came Wild Dog, his
coat all sludgy and muddy.

"Such ugly clothes," murmured
Hog, admiring his own fine coat.
Wild Dog snarled and left.

And even when beautiful Cheetah
came down to drink, Hog stared at
the dark black marks under her eyes
and murmured, "Miserable-faced
people should stay at home."

Cheetah hissed and quickly
walked away.

Handsome Hog was smiling happily at his reflection when at him. Lion was looking cross, Wild Dog was They were all coming straight at him. and ran. And Lion and Cheetah

he noticed that the other animals were looking even more cross and Cheetah was crosser still.

"Uh oh!" said Handsome Hog. He turned and Wild Dog began to chase him.

They chased him past the tall
twisted Thorn Trees.
They chased him through the dry
and prickly Burr Bushes.

They chased him under the
Wait-a-bit Thorns.

And they even chased him
through the Sticky Swamp.

But Hog ran and ran, and finally when
he saw his new home he rushed
down the hole...

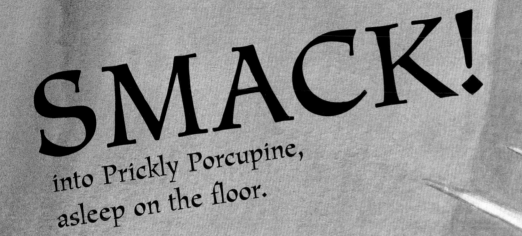

SMACK!

into Prickly Porcupine,
asleep on the floor.

"Oouch!"

Hog yelled as hundreds
of prickles punctured
him. He turned
and ran out again.

When Lion and Cheetah and
Wild Dog saw Handsome Hog
run out of the hole, they
laughed so much they forgot
to chase him any more.

His tail was sticking straight
up in the air, stiff as a stick,
and his face was all swollen
and full of prickles.

Hog went to the river to gaze
at his reflection. But his tail
was still sticking straight up in
the air! And his face had large
warty, bumpy lumps!

"Warty Hog!
Warty Hog!"
the animals
began to chant.

And Warthog he has
been called ever since.

And, nowadays, Warthog is careful
to choose an empty hole to live in.

And once he has made a fine wide tunnel, he always
goes into it slowly and carefully and...

...backwards!